MR GARDEN

ILLUSTRATED BY
JANE PATON

MR GARDEN

ELEANOR FARJEON

HENRY Z. WALCK.INC.,NEW YORK

First American edition 1966
Library of Congress Catalog Card Number: 66–13951

Second impression August 1966

© 1965 THE EXECUTORS OF THE LATE
ELEANOR FARJEON

Illustrations © 1966 JANE PATON

Printed in Great Britain
by W. S. Cowell Ltd, The Butter Market,
Ipswich, England.

I

Harry came into the room and said, "A man has come."

I looked up from reading a cross letter from a neighbour. "Bother, who is he?"

"We just said Hullo. He hasn't got a name I dare say."

Angela was stretched on her stomach on the carpet where she was examining a spread-out newspaper. "Everybody's got a name," she said. "That's who they *are*." She turned to me. "Mummy, it isn't in the paper!"

"He's a very little man," Harry went on, holding up an envelope. "Can I have this stamp from abroad, Mummy?"

"How little?" Angela asked.

I said, "Look more carefully, Angela, it *must* be there. Don't touch the letters, Harry, you shall have it presently."

"He's as little as a bird," said Harry. "Is presently now or tomorrow?"

190693

"Do you mean a sparrow or an ostrich?" asked Angela.

"I mean as a blackbird."

"Nobody is as little as a blackbird."

"Yes he is, if he's as little as a blackbird that's as big as he is."

"Now you're just being silly."

"Well I don't care, I like him, he's different."

"How's he different?"

"His boots are different."

"Different boots to your boots?"

"Different boots to themselves. One of them's a sandshoe."

"Well I can't find it," said Angela. "The print's too small."

I sighed. "Oh dear! If the advertisement's not in this week we'll have to wait till next Friday."

Angela continued tracing the local paper with her finger. "Mr Carpenter will get a whole week crosser about the dandelions if a man doesn't come soon."

"He's come now," said Harry. "I told you."

I laid down my neighbour's letter. "What has he come for, Harry?"

"To weed the garden."

I flew down to the door, Harry on my heels.

The man who had come was bigger than a blackbird, but he *was* very little. Two bright blue eyes peered at me out of a lot of tawny hair. I glanced at his feet. A soiled plimsoll with a much-knotted shoestring was on one of them, the other wore

a cracked black boot too big for it. My glance hastened up-wards to the glistening eyes again; it dared not loiter on what the little man was (or wasn't) wearing in between his feet and his hair. He was smiling toothlessly, but I liked the smile.

7

"My little boy says—" I hesitated. "Is it about the garden?"

"That's it. Your garden do want a gardener, don't it?" He said this like a statement, not a question.

"You saw my advertisement then?"

He answered indirectly, "I looked over the fence."

"Have you brought any tools?" He shook his head slightly. "But you *are* a—I mean, you do understand gardens?"

"That's it, I understand 'em. I was born in a wood."

Harry chimed in eagerly, "In the very middle?"

"Thereabouts."

"What is your name?" I asked.

He didn't seem to notice this. I wondered how I could approach the question of references. But Harry had taken his hand fondly. "I'm going to call you Mr Garden. I'll show you where the toolshed is."

"*Wait* a moment, Harry!" How on earth would Mr Garden tackle my eighth of an acre of sowthistle and bindweed? Anyhow, what arrangement had we come to? But they didn't wait. I watched them go, helplessly. They were almost of a height. Harry is tall for eight years old, and Mr Garden was short for—what? Thirty? Fifty? I gave it up.

Angela came downstairs with the folded newspaper. "It *is* in, Mummy, I've spotted it. Who's that?"

"It's Mr Garden."

"Oh! Is he going to do the weeds?"

"He seems to think so."

Angela considered his back view. "D'you think he *can*?"

"That's what I'm wondering. We'd better go and see."

We trailed behind them into the heart of my twelve-
months' jungle. Harry was explaining it.

"That's the rosebed, I mean it was last year when we were
abroad. That's the herbitious border, lupins aren't any good in
omelettes though. I picked Emily some one day when there
wasn't any parsley, and she said did I want to be poisoned.
This is where the rockery is somewhere. Rock-roses look more
like buttercups I think. Here's where my *very own* bit of garden is, right underneath, it begins *here* and goes on for twenty-
two-and-a-half inches to *there*. I measured it with a tape-
measure."

"I see." Mr Garden stooped to lift a curtain of chickweed,
peering. I felt it was time for me to do some talking.

"Doesn't all this frighten you?"

He smiled his toothless smile.

"You think you can tackle it?"

"That's it."

"Come every day," said Harry.

"Twice a week'll do," said Mr Garden.

Angela addressed him rather coldly. "I expect you read my mother's advert, it said two days."

"Never done much reading." Mr Garden's glance passed across her and back to Harry. "We'll get your piece going first, chap."

"We haven't quite settled yet, have we?" I ventured. "What do you—?"

"Three-and-ninepence an hour."

"Funny price," remarked Angela. I nudged her to be quiet.

"You're·sure that suits you, Mr Garden?" It was half the usual wage. He nodded. I said, "Oh, and by the way, your address is—? Just in case—"

Harry cut across me, saying, "Some weeds I don't like, but some I do. Why are daisies flowers in fields and weeds in lawns?"

"Any daisies we find we'll leave," said Mr Garden. He gave Harry the trowel and took the spade. Angela and I, unwanted, returned to the house.

Emily was looking out of the kitchen window. She is long-sighted and observant, and misses nothing.

"Have you taken him on, ma'am?"

"I seem to have."

"He may do all right."

"I hope I haven't made a mistake, Emily. I don't know his name or where he lives."

"This time of year they live out."

"Who do?"

"Him and his likes. They sleep in in winter, in summer save their money. You'll see them coming off the Heath in the morning to get a cuppa before they start looking for a job. You can tell by their clothes when they've been sleeping out. Will he be here all day, or just the half?"

"I don't know."

"Will I make him some tea?"

"Yes, of course, and some cheese or something."

"Righty-ho," said Emily.

We went upstairs. "It's three-farthings a minute," said Angela.

"What is?"

"Three-and-ninepence an hour."

"Did you do that in your head?"

"Well I had to. I'm going to practise my arpeggios now. What are you going to do?"

"Write to Mr Carpenter and tell him we've got a gardener, and I hope my dandelions won't upset him any more."

I wrote my letter to the background music of Angela's piano practice. I never have to tell her when to do it. She is as methodical and single-purposed as an ant. Harry, who tries and sometimes manages to escape practice of any sort, always seems to me as methodless as a butterfly. But perhaps the purpose of the ant on its anthill is more obvious than the hither-and-thither of a butterfly in the air. He came in late for lunch with most of his garden under his fingernails.

190693

"Go and wash," said Angela.

"Must I, Mummy?"

"Never mind for this once, the soup will get cold. Have you enjoyed your morning?"

"Yes, thank you. I know how to catch slugs and Mr Garden's going to show me how to bud roses, and he's divided the strawberries and we'll have twice as many next year, and I'm going to plant one in my garden. I'll plant one of everything, I dare say. Is it presently yet?"

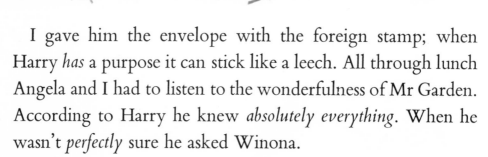

I gave him the envelope with the foreign stamp; when Harry *has* a purpose it can stick like a leech. All through lunch Angela and I had to listen to the wonderfulness of Mr Garden. According to Harry he knew *absolutely everything*. When he wasn't *perfectly* sure he asked Winona.

"Who's Winona?" asked Angela.

"She's the goddess of the wind. They're tremendous friends. He stands still and spreads his arms out like this, and his fingers sort of play five-finger exercises, like this. That's how he found the lily-bulbs."

"What lily-bulbs, Harry?"

"In the dip down by the fence."

"But we've never had any lily-bulbs there, or anywhere."

"I helped him pull them up, hundreds and thousands of them! Mr Garden's potted them down in the shed for next year. He's going to plant them both sides of the middle path, and in July they'll simply *rush* up like armies of tigers, all striped and gnashing their teeth at us!"

"No they won't," said Angela.

"Why won't they?"

"Because they're Flora, not Fauna."

"I don't know what you mean," said Harry.

"And I don't believe about Winona either."

Harry subsided sulkily into his plate of floating island. It is his favourite pudding, and Emily always sees that he has it on Fridays. On Tuesdays Angela has her treacle tart. She likes things she can get her teeth into.

After lunch I went out to look at the jungle, and was staggered by the difference Mr Garden had made in half a day. Only a small portion of it was cleared, but almost all of it showed signs of order to come. A mind had been brought to bear on chaos, and Mr Garden's arms and legs had obeyed it with passion. He was drinking tea and munching a thick sandwich; there was a chunk of cake on the tray Emily had brought out to him.

"How do you find it, Mr Garden?"

"I've seen worse. Ground wants lime, full of leather jackets."

"Can you get some?"

"They know me at Spiller's."

"Then will you? They can charge it to me. My little boy tells me you've found a lot of bulbs."

"*Ar!*" His eyes glittered under his loose hair. He traced the air above what was once the centre path, now matted with couch-grass. "We'll have 'em along there, very tall, two rows, up to the bird-bath. I'll clean that out."

"They'll look splendid, Mr Garden." Under his fingers playing on the air I saw strips of velvet grass bordered with flaming ranks of lilies, and at the end of this vista a snow-white basin filled with a flurry of feathers, brown, blue, grey, scattering sparkling showers against the rich background of our copper beech. "But I simply can't think where they came from."

He smiled his smile. "You wasn't here, little chap says." He mumbled his last mouthful of Emily's cake. "Lot happens in a year."

"Yes, I suppose it does. Will you be staying on this afternoon?" He nodded.

Mr Garden stayed his full eight hours. I gave him thirty shillings, hoping he would find a lodging with some of it. Emily thought not, and she wasn't sure he would be back on Monday.

"Why not?"

"They go sudden."

"Where to?"

Emily shrugged. "Just go."

II

But Mr Garden did come back on Monday. He appeared
punctually at eight o'clock and went at five. Between twelve
and one he lunched in the toolshed, then roamed round,
pondering, playing the air with his fingers, staring at what was
before him, and at what wasn't.

Harry dashed out to join him after lessons, and seemed to
spend the rest of the summer in his company. At our mealtimes
there was always a new tale of the marvels we would have in
the garden next year. Oceans of white and yellow and orange
poppies—"They'll come from Iceland, by reindeer I dare say"
—and a lavender walk, to bring the bees. Bees meant more
flowers, and flowers meant more honey, and honey meant
more bees. "There might be a million actually, this time next
year."

"Then we shan't be able to go in the garden ourselves," said
Angela.

"Oh, they don't sting you if you know how to handle them. Yesterday one fell in the bird-bath and Mr Garden saved its life with his fingers, and it just dried itself and flew into a hollyhock. Mummy, d'you know, a *bird* sat on my wrist today and pecked some cheese out of my hand. Mr Garden does it when he has his lunch, just sits with his hand out full of crumbs, and makes bird-noises, and they come. You must keep your hand as still as a twig. When he lived in the wood a chaffinch who was his friend sat on his head and pulled out some hairs to make a nest with. Mr Garden's going to mend up that there old garden frame with polythene sheets or something, and fill it with simply hundreds of little flower-pots with cucumber and marrow seeds, and why not melons, Mr Garden says. Why not, Mummy?"

Why not, indeed? It became more evident from week to week that we had acquired a gardener to whom gardening was a vocation. I went out to talk to him about melons, and took him a faded cardigan and a pair of boots that matched. Emily had a range of male relations she often spoke about, whom we'd never seen. Soon Mr Garden was wearing Emily's

Cousin Frank's check shirt, and her Uncle Bob's socks and braces. Harry insisted on contributing his own red-and-blue muffler. Mr Garden accepted these offerings with simplicity, but while he was willing to wear Emily's brother-in-law's green tie, he firmly rejected that gentleman's bowler hat. Headgear of any sort was taboo.

20

"He likes Winona to breathe through his hair," explained Harry. "Her breathing is full of scents and smells, he says."

"Smells!" sniffed Angela.

"Mr Garden says they're all of a piece, you can't expect to have roses without bemure."

"Bemure, Harry?"

"Dung," said Harry. "Horse-dung's as precious as gold-dust these here days. I'm going to get a bag and look for some. When Mr Garden was my age he had a little sack, and scraped it up off the roads, and sold it to the gentry-folk for tuppence. You can't do that any more, because motor-cars don't."

The cast-off—I forget whose—that pleased Mr Garden most were some corduroy trousers, so threadbare that you had to guess what the colour had once been. They looked like the earth he knelt in. He turned up the ends with safety-pins.

21

On my birthday I received an exciting present by air from a friend in Honolulu. She had flown me a parcel of the strangest flowers we had ever seen. Their shapes were as violent as their colours were vivid. They hung out scarlet tongues like snakes from their fleshy heads, and thrust at you with harsh green blades like knives.

"More artificial than real," commented Emily.

"Not in Honolulu," said Angela. "The Honolulans would probably think bluebells are artificial."

"Can I show them to Mr Garden before you put them in vases?" asked Harry, and bore them away. He came back rather quickly, looking scared. "Mummy, he said don't you bring them things out here, not if you don't want serpents in Eden, he said."

"Did he *really* say that, Harry?"

"Yes, and he walked round and round the bird-bath, muttering to Winona. Here they are, Mummy, I'm afraid I dropped the purple one with the yellow warts and trod on it and it squashed, so I had to throw it away."

"Never mind." I put the strange creatures in the big vase in the hall.

Summer drew out, autumn drew in. Twice weekly Mr Garden swept up more and more leaves as he cleared the beds of their past glories. At lunch Harry announced, "We're going to have an absolutely *enormous* bonfire!"

When I went to pay Mr Garden his money, he was leaning on his broom in the middle of the lawn. His blue eyes roamed here and there, dwelling on the tidy paths and the ordered earth.

"Very different from when you came to us, Mr Garden."

"Ar." He smiled his smile. "Not enough to do now, two full days. Shall I make it two halfs?"

I felt rather troubled. "But how will you—I mean, can you manage on two half-days a week?"

"Just about, time being."

But I hadn't meant could he manage the garden; I meant could he manage to live as the garden died. Its life was his living. The nights were chilly now for sleeping out.

III

We had the bonfire two weeks later. Not on one of Mr
Garden's Mondays or Thursdays. He appeared on Saturday
when the wind was favourable, and the drift of smoke
wouldn't upset our neighbour. Was it Winona who had supplied
this day of mellow light and soft still air? The vapours arose in
faint spirals from the first pale flames, and when the crackling
garbage became a blaze, the fumes from the smoke-clouds
flowed away from Mr Carpenter's side of the fence.

Harry ran excitedly to and fro, renewing the fires with handfuls of litter stored up during the past weeks. We all came out to help and to enjoy.

"Here's some more!" shouted Angela, thrusting thin sticks below the smouldering ash.

"Don't scorch yourself," warned Emily, flinging leaves.

I brought the faded remains of Honolulu to the sacrifice, and saw them coil and shrivel without regret. Mr Garden trod them down fiercely; they spat at him as, arms outspread, his fingers drummed the air. The scents and smells of bygone summer

blew through his hair. Only he and Harry knew the origin of
every armful of refuse that went to the flames. It was Adam
who delved and lit the bonfires of Eden. We women went
back to the house to make the tea. We brought it out to our
men, and sat on the ground round the fire at a respectful
distance from the heat. Harry sat next to Mr Garden sniffing
the smoke.

"It was gorgeous!" exclaimed Angela with flushed cheeks.

"You've burnt your boots," said Emily, pouring tea.

"Ar!" said Mr Garden, munching cake.

I doubled his wage when he left. He pocketed it without comment. On Monday he didn't come. There was nothing to be done about it. He had no address, and we had never known his name.

IV

After Christmas we left Emily in charge as usual, and went abroad again to our friends who lived in the sun. We had only meant to stay through the English winter, but I fell ill and my friends insisted on nursing me till I was fit to travel. So we did not come back until the middle of spring. Harry's first question to Emily was, "Is Mr Garden here?"

"You'll know if you go and look," said Emily.

He turned quickly, but she called him back from the door. "Don't go disappointing yourself. I only meant you'd know he wasn't here by the state the garden's in."

We all went out to look.

"Oh dear!" I said. "I must advertise again and hope for the best."

It was the worst who came. They said they understood gardens. One of them spent a morning digging up the circle of cloth of gold wallflowers with which Mr Garden had framed a deep pool of forget-me-nots. They weren't in flower yet, and he assured me they were weeds. Another I stopped in the nick of time from chopping my pet apple-tree in half. He said

he was a champion pruner, and half a tree would give me twice as many apples twice as big. As I couldn't keep my eye on him all the time I gave it up, stopped advertising, and let the weeds flourish rather than destroy the beautiful things that were happening among them week after week.

The golden fountains of forsythia, the flood of primroses
and windflowers outnumbering the chickweed, an aviary of
parrot tulips that vied with the dandelions, in every corner
flowers we had never dreamed of that came and went as spring
moved on into summer. Then the roses took our breath away.
Day by day Harry was first man out to discover and announce
fresh wonders. Carnations like ballet-dancers in frilled scarlet

skirts among the lupins, a melon-flower in the mended frame, bees humming like audible sunshine over cushions of lavender, and one day he ran in shouting "Tiger-lilies! Tiger-lilies!" Yes, there they were, two exciting rows of them—and the air about them was choked with dandelion clocks. Next morning's post brought a letter from Mr Carpenter.

"Funny," said Angela.

"What is?" asked Harry.

"This is the exact date it came last year."

"How do you know?"

"I put it in my diary." She brought the book to show us. "Here it is—'Mr Carpenter wrote to Mummy about the dandelions, and Mr Garden came.'"

Harry rushed back to the jungle, shouting, "Mr Garden!"

I looked at Emily, clearing the table, filled with a strange hope.

Emily said, "It might be."

Angela ran after Harry. We all felt it might be.

But it was not. The children haunted the garden all day, and went to bed tired with disappointment.

I wrote an apologetic note to Mr Carpenter, and drafted one more advertisement to the local paper.

"Perhaps he'll see it and come," said Angela.

"He didn't see it last time," said Harry. "He just knew. There's nothing for him to know now."

I thought my little boy looked rather strained.

The advertisement brought one answer, a man I didn't feel I could trust the garden to.

"Must we have him, Mummy?"

"I hope not—but the dandelions are dreadful."

"Something is more dreadful," muttered Harry.

"What do you mean, Harry?"

"I mean, I mean"—He went slowly, almost reluctantly, into the garden. We followed him to the glowing rose bushes. In their midst, gloating over them like a triumphant enemy, towered a fleshy purple monster, spotted with yellow. The big garden spade lay fallen beside it.

"Ugh!" shuddered Angela.

Emily said, "My goodness."

"I can't dig it up," said Harry. "The roots go down and down to the middle of the world, as thick as elephant trunks. It must be the one I threw away. It didn't get burned with the others."

"*Ar!* That's it."

36

Mr Garden was looking over the fence. Mr Garden with odd boots on his feet, his clothes more tattered than ever, except for the threadbare earth-coloured corduroys. Mr Garden, his blue eyes glittering with wrath, the wind blowing his loose hair in tawny flames all round his head. Mr Garden looking like the Avenging Archangel Michael.

He climbed the fence and stooped for the big spade.
"Get your trowel, chap," he said to Harry.

We went back to the house, leaving them to it. Angela made an entry in her diary. I sat down and wrote a note to Mr Carpenter. Emily hotted the teapot and began to cut sandwiches.

J E
F228m   190693

          Farjeon
          Mr. Gardon.